STAR WARS™

ADVENTURES IN WILD SPACE

THE STEAL

READ MORE
ADVENTURES IN WILD SPACE

Prelude: THE ESCAPE
Book 1: THE SNARE
Book 2: THE NEST
Book 4: THE DARK

EGMONT
We bring stories to life

First published in Great Britain 2016
by Egmont UK Limited, The Yellow Building,
1 Nicholas Road, London W11 4AN

Illustrations by David M. Buisán
Designed by Richie Hull
Typesetting by Janene Spencer

© & ™ 2016 Lucasfilm Ltd.

ISBN 978 1 4052 7995 6
62727/1

Printed in UK

To find more great *Star Wars* books, visit
www.egmont.co.uk/starwars

CAVAN SCOTT

A long time ago in a galaxy far, far away . . . .

ADVENTURES IN
WILD SPACE
T H E   S T E A L

As the evil Emperor Palpatine
strengthens his iron grip on the galaxy,
Lina and *Milo Graf* search for their
missing parents, kidnapped by Captain
Korda of the Imperial Navy.

*Travelling on board the WHISPER BIRD
with their trusted droid CR-8R, the
children have learned the source of a
mysterious transmission that is calling
for a rebellion against the Empire itself.
Their course is set for the planet Lothal.*

*Little do Lina and Milo know that
sinister forces are closing in, greedy
for the secret information lodged in
CR-8R's memory banks . . . .*

CHAPTER 1

SHADY BUSINESS

Captain Korda scowled at the viewport in front of him. The swirling crimson eye of a gas giant stared back.

To Korda's right, an Imperial officer nervously approached him, brandishing a datapad.

'Captain, we have the latest findings for you.'

He was a pathetic-looking specimen, with a fleshy, pockmarked face and a belly that put considerable strain on his grey uniform.

'And you are?'

The young officer swallowed.

'Junior Lieutenant Jams, sir.'

Korda snatched the pad from a shaking hand.

'Your uniform is a disgrace, Jams. Those boots look like they haven't been cleaned in months, your collar is filthy and your insignia is crooked.'

Jams looked nervously down at the rank plaque on his chest; two red squares sat on top of two blue. His pudgy hand went to adjust the pins, but he hesitated, thinking better of it.

'I'm sorry, sir. I'll do better.'

'See that you do,' Korda growled, slapping the pad against Jams's chest. 'Come onto my bridge looking like that again and you'll wish you never went to the Imperial Academy.'

'Yes, sir,' Jams stuttered, almost dropping the pad before he scuttled off. 'Thank you, sir.'

Korda sighed. How had it come

to this? Not that long ago he'd been the rising star of the Imperial Navy, receiving medals of commendation from Governor Tarkin and receiving missions from Lord Vader himself. Now, he was cataloguing gas giants on the edge of Wild Space in a near-obsolete star-freighter. The boredom was crippling, days filled with pointless scans and tedious reports. Even bullying his pathetic excuse for a crew had lost its joy.

He rubbed the puckered skin around his metal jaw. The scarred flesh itched terribly, another reminder of his failure. All this disgrace was down to two children – Lina and Milo Graf. It had seemed such a simple mission. Arrest cartographers Auric and Rhyssa Graf, and confiscate their extensive archive of planetary maps. How was he to know that the woman would trick them, hiding the data on a droid, or that the two Graf brats would evade capture so skilfully? Korda could still hear Lord Vader's words when he'd made his report.

'*You let the children escape?*'

Korda had been lucky to get out of the briefing with his life.

This would not stand. He wouldn't spend the rest of his career out here in the wastes.

He marched across the bridge, only to find his way blocked by an ensign with dark skin and a worried expression.

'Sir, we are scheduled for another seven hours around Klytus V...'

Korda stepped around the young fool, heading for the doors. 'Then you won't be needing me, Ensign. I'll expect a full report at the end of your shift. Do you understand?'

'Yes sir,' the Ensign replied as he watched Korda stalk from the bridge.

* * *

Korda swept into his private quarters and locked the door behind him. He pulled off his cap and threw it across the cramped cabin onto the bed. Sitting in front of a tiny holoprojector, he tapped his private access code into the computer and opened the secret comms-channel he'd been using for the last few weeks.

If he was to regain his honour, he needed news, and quickly.

The holoprojector beeped as it established a connection, piggybacking Korda's signal on the back of official Imperial communications.

Finally, after what seemed like an eternity, a translucent image appeared

in the air before Korda. The Captain
found himself looking into the glowing
eyes of a masked figure, who glowered
back at him from beneath a heavy cowl.

'*Captain, this is not a convenient
time.*'

'I've told you not to use my rank on
an open channel,' Korda snapped.
'And I'll decide whether it's convenient

or not.'

The hologram inclined its head. '*Of course, sir.*'

Better. It was about time he was shown some respect.

'What have you discovered?'

'*I am following a lead.*'

This was like pulling teeth from a bantha. 'Where?'

'*That doesn't concern you.*'

'Doesn't concern me? I'm the one *paying* you!'

'*And the reason my fee is so high is that you insisted on complete discretion. After all, a respected Imperial officer hiring a bounty hunter? Whatever would your superiors think?*'

Korda struggled to keep his temper in check. The bounty hunter was mocking him, but unfortunately was also right. By employing the Shade, one of the most notorious mercenaries

in the Outer Rim, Korda was breaking
every rule in the book. But the prize
was worth it. If the Shade could find
the Grafs' maps, Korda could use
the data to make a series of startling
discoveries in Wild Space. High
Command would welcome him back
with open arms if he unearthed a new
energy source or precious metal.

And if he saw off the Graf children
in the process, well, that would be a
bonus.

'Very well. I'll expect a report–'

'*Understood,*' the Shade replied,
terminating the communication. The
hologram vanished, leaving Korda
fuming in silence.

Once he was back where he
belonged, he would take great pleasure
in executing the bounty hunter in the
Emperor's name.

* * *

Thousands of light years away, the Shade slapped shut a wrist-mounted holo-receiver.

The bounty hunter stepped out of a ramshackle porch and looked up and down the narrow alley. It was empty, although the sounds of the neighbouring street could be heard. This was Skree, a century-old space-station hidden in the middle of a dust nebula. Away from the Empire's prying eyes, it attracted the worst scum in the galaxy. The Shade felt right at home.

The cloaked bounty hunter swept down the alley. It was almost time for the rendezvous. Reaching a corner, the Shade peeked around, seeing a tall red-skinned male by the name of Meggin. The alien had taken the Shade's bait, the promise of a lead for

his treasure-loving boss. Perfect.

Looking around nervously, Meggin walked into the tumbledown tavern as arranged. That was the Shade's cue. The bounty hunter crossed the busy street, following Meggin into the crumbling building. The alien was inside, looking around in confusion. The bar was empty – just as the Shade had arranged.

Meggin turned, his small, sunken eyes widening as he took in the small black sphere in the Shade's gloved hand. With a flick of the bounty hunter's wrist the sphere shot through the air towards Meggin, hitting the alien in the chest and pinning him to the wall like a Sriluurian butterfly mounted on a board.

'Struggle as much as you like,' the Shade told him, stalking forward. 'You're trapped in a localised force field. Not even a gundark could break free of its grip.'

'What do you want?' stammered Meggin.

'Information,' came the reply. A hologram of two children filled the air. 'Milo and Lina Graf – where are they?'

Meggin shook his head. 'I don't know who they are!'

'That's a lie,' the Shade said calmly. 'Shall we try again?'

The mercenary stabbed a button on the wrist-mounted comlink. Meggin cried out in pain as the metal orb pressed harder against his chest.

'I've just increased the gravitational pressure of the sphere. It will continue to crush you until you tell the truth.'

Still the red-skinned alien refused to answer. The Shade pressed the control again, and Meggin gasped in discomfort. It was only a matter of time.

* * *

Just under fifteen minutes later, the Shade strode out of the tavern. The bounty hunter had the answer and was already planning a route to the Outer Rim.

The Graf children were heading to Lothal, and the Shade would be waiting.

CHAPTER 2

LOTHAL

Lina Graf sat back in the *Whisper Bird*'s flight chair and looked at the blue and green planet that lay ahead of them.

So that was Lothal.

It looked so peaceful, clouds swirling across its surface. She had almost forgotten what peaceful felt like. The last week had seen her life turned upside down. Since her parents had been captured by the Galactic Empire, Lina and her brother Milo had escaped stormtroopers, TIE fighters and slobbering monsters. No wonder she felt so tired. Right now, all she wanted

was to roll up in a ball and go to sleep –
but that wouldn't help find their parents,
would it?

The navicomputer beeped. The
Whisper Bird would be entering Lothal's
atmosphere within a few minutes.

At least the ship was operating
properly for once. The *Bird* had always
been temperamental – held together
by a mixture of obsolete tech and good
luck – but had taken a real beating over
the last few days. Lina had pushed
the hyperdrive to the limits and every
system seemed on the point of collapse.
She glanced at the fault locator on the
central console. No lights were flashing.
No alarms sounding. Perhaps that's
why she was feeling uneasy. Was she
getting used to exploding circuits and
emergency repairs?

Certainly, the journey to Lothal had
been surprisingly free from crisis. They

had dropped Sata and Meggin off in the Skree nebula, and followed the signals they had first picked up on Thune.

Lina's fingers ran along the comms-control as she tried to find the frequency, hidden among official Imperial communications. At first there was static, but then she heard a snatch of the now familiar voice. It was a man, speaking close to a microphone.

'They say they have our best interests at heart, but it's not true. Every day more people vanish. The Empire is lying to us. They are...'

The voice distorted and was lost in a burst of white noise, the connection broken. It didn't matter. Meggin had told Lina and Milo that the transmissions came from Lothal's Capital City. Perhaps whoever was making the broadcasts could help them find their parents – or know someone who could.

It was a long shot, but they were running out of options.

Lina pushed the *Whisper Bird*'s engines just that little bit more.

They were almost there.

From somewhere behind her, there was a loud crash followed by an electronic wail.

'Milo?' Lina cried out, jumping from her seat to race from the cockpit. 'What was that? Is it the gravity compensators? Have they overloaded?'

The only answer she received was a sharp yell from her younger brother. 'Look out!'

'Milo?'

She barrelled into the living quarters and ducked as something zoomed overhead.

In front of her, Milo was rolling around the floor... in fits of laughter!

She ducked again as the heavy

object swept over her head. It was their droid, CR-8R, his repulsors firing on all cylinders.

'Get it off me!' the droid screeched, before banging into the far wall.

'Get what off you?' Lina asked, before spotting a wiry Kowakian monkey-lizard clamped around the droid's head. The small creature was cackling as CR-8R tried to prise it off with flailing arms.

'Morq!' Lina yelled and the monkey-lizard's head snapped up to stare at her. It let out a panicked yelp and leapt from CR-8R's head to hide behind the still-sniggering Milo. CR-8R, meanwhile, crashed into the holo-table and came to a stop on his side.

'What are you doing?' Lina said, her hands on her hips.

'Just having a little fun,' Milo laughed.

'Fun?' exclaimed CR-8R, righting himself. 'That flea-bag almost ripped out my audio-receptors.'

'Well, you did say you couldn't stand the sound of Morq's voice!' Milo responded, the monkey-lizard peeking guiltily over his shoulder. 'He was just putting his fingers in your ears for you!'

Lina couldn't believe this. She'd honestly believed something was wrong with the ship. Instead, it had all just been another squabble between their droid and Milo's pet!

'We haven't got time for this,' she insisted. 'We're on the final approach to Lothal. Crater needs to transmit a fake ID so the Imperials don't realise we're the *Whisper Bird.*'

'I remember when I used to tell *you* what to do,' CR-8R said haughtily, hovering away from the holo-table.

'She just likes to think she's in charge,' commented Milo, tickling Morq under the chin.

'Someone has to be the sensible one round here,' Lina snapped at her brother. 'Why don't you make yourself useful and keep quiet!'

She turned to stalk back to the cockpit, knowing full well that Milo would be sticking out his tongue at her back. Morq was probably joining in!

She didn't care. At least CR-8R was already in position, connecting to the *Bird*'s computer. Ahead of them, an Imperial freighter orbited Lothal, but CR-8R's supply of false identities would fool the Imperials into giving them permission to land.

Probably.

* * *

Thankfully, the false ID worked like a charm and the *Whisper Bird* was soon swooping down through Lothal's bright blue sky.

Milo and Morq had joined them in the cockpit, the earlier argument already forgotten at the sight that lay ahead.

A city of gleaming towers sat on the horizon, each skyscraper rising majestically from the ground like a glistening needle.

'That's where we're heading?' Milo asked.

'Capital City,' Lina confirmed.

'It's beautiful,' Milo said. 'Although what's *that* supposed to be?'

He was pointing past the skyscrapers to a partially constructed black dome. Large cranes supported the structure as a cluster of chimneys belched thick smoke into the atmosphere.

'The new Imperial base,' CR-8R

reported. 'Lothal invited the Empire here three months ago. According to the local news channel, Lothal is to be the centre of a new hyperspace route, providing safe passage across the galaxy.'

Milo looked at the vast tracts of farmland below them. Massive automated machines were ripping up the crops, clearing hectares and hectares of cereal.

'Looks like the Empire wants more than a hyper-way.'

'Lothal is rich in minerals. I would think those farms are being cleared for mining,' said CR-8R.

Lina frowned. The Imperial dome looked like a monster looming up behind the graceful spires of Capital City. It didn't belong.

'Is that where we're heading?' Milo asked, indicating a busy space-port to the right of the city.

Lina shook her head. 'I wish. I've booked us into a cheap landing strip on the other side of the city. It'll be a bit of a walk.'

Milo sighed. 'Because we want to keep a low profile?'

'No, because we're running low on credits. Capital City is an expensive place to visit.'

'Which may cause another problem,' added CR-8R.

'Which is?' Lina asked, not wanted to hear any more bad news.

The droid tapped a gauge on the dashboard. 'Our fuel reserves are also dangerously low. If we don't replenish the fuel cells soon, we may not be able to even take off again'

'Let's worry about one thing at a time,' Lina cut in. 'I can see the landing strip.'

Milo followed his sister's gaze out of

the cockpit windows.

'That's it?' he said. The *Whisper Bird* had swept around the skyscrapers and was heading for a clump of squat, run-down buildings a kilometre or so from Capital City. In the middle of the shanty town lay a narrow strip of brown earth dotted with equally decrepit ships.

'It's all we can afford,' Lina reminded him. 'I'm taking us in.'

With Lina at the controls, the *Whisper Bird* made a perfect touch-down, soft clay

bubbling around its landing pads.

'And you're sure the ship's not just going to sink into the ground?' Milo said as they gingerly walked down the *Bird*'s ramp.

'I'm not sure of anything,' Lina admitted, glancing around at their surroundings. Aliens were everywhere, milling around the ships or lounging outside the rickety buildings. Lina had the unsettling impression that all eyes were on them.

'I suggest we keep moving,' CR-8R piped up. 'Some of these characters look distinctly unsavoury. I think I'd rather spend more time with Morq than hang around here!'

They traipsed across the muddy excuse for a landing strip, heading towards a road that led towards the City.

'What about the transmission?' Milo

asked the droid. 'Can you track it?'

CR-8R cocked his head as they passed the first buildings. 'I can't even detect it anymore. Our mysterious rebel seems to have stopped broad...'

The droid's voice dropped away as a huge creature stepped in front of them. It was almost twice the size of Lina, a walking wall of muscle, with scaly skin, a cluster of tiny eyes beneath a solitary brow and drool flowing from a wide lip-less mouth.

'Nice ship,' the colossus growled, with a voice that sounded as if it could easily shake planets apart.

'T-thanks,' stammered Lina, grabbing Milo's arm to try to manoeuvre her brother around the non-human. 'We like it.'

The hulking alien blocked their way. 'I like too. I take it.'

'The *Whisper Bird* is not for sale,'

CR-8R informed him haughtily, and the alien grinned, showing stubs of yellow teeth.

'Sell? You give to me!'

'Is that right?' said an accented voice from behind them. The children turned to see another alien glaring at the other with hooded, blood-red eyes. This one was tall, his powerful frame draped in a long, heavy cape with a large hood rested

on the two pointed horns on his head.

The muscled bully backed away instantly.

'S-sorry,' it stuttered, multiple eyes wide with panic. 'My mistake. Thought you someone else.'

The creature turned and fled, faster than Lina would have thought possible.

'T-thanks,' said Lina, regarding the newcomer with what she considered a healthy level of trepidation.

'Not a problem,' he replied. 'This is not a safe place for children. You should come with me.'

CR-8R put a mechanical hand on Lina's shoulder. 'Thank you for the kind offer, but I am sure we will be just fine on our own.'

The droid started guiding Milo and Lina away.

'Of course,' the horned alien said, waving them goodbye. 'After all, it's not like you need help finding your transmission.'

Milo turned back to the alien who was grinning like a Danorian wolf. 'How do you know we're even looking for one?'

The alien pulled down his hood to reveal two pointed ears, each furnished with gold rings.

'Couldn't help but overhear, kid,' he rumbled. 'The question is whether you're going to trust me or not?'

Lina took a tentative step forward. 'You can take us to the person who's making the transmissions?'

The alien's smirk grew wider. 'Not personally, but I know someone who can help. For the right price, of course.'

'And how much is that?' Lina said, trying to keep the quiver from her voice.

The alien poked the tip of a pink tongue through sharp teeth. 'That's something you need to ask my boss.'

'Your boss?' parroted CR-8R. 'We

don't even know who you are, sir!'

'I apologise. How rude of me.' The alien gave a mock bow. 'Cikatro Vizago at your service.'

CHAPTER 3

CRATE EXPECTATIONS

'Are you sure this is a good idea?' Milo asked as they flew along the road to Capital City.

'No,' Lina replied. After making the introductions, Vizago had bundled the children and CR-8R onto the back of a landspeeder which was now whizzing away from the landing strip. 'But what choice did we have?'

'We could have got back in the ship and flown away,' CR-8R replied. 'If we hadn't wasted all our fuel getting here in the first place.'

'It won't be a waste if it can help us find Mum and Dad,' Lina scolded him.

Vizago looked over his shoulder. 'Who's that you're trying to find?'

'It doesn't matter,' Lina said, not wanting to reveal too many secrets to the horned stranger. 'We just need to find out who's behind those transmissions.'

Vizago laughed. 'That's what everyone wants to know. Especially the Imperials. Old Azadi is running out of time.'

'Who?' asked Milo, shifting towards the pilot.

'Him!' said Vizago, indicating a large holo-screen on the side of a skyscraper. The face of a stern man glared back at them. 'Ryder Azadi, Governor of Lothal. The Empire's given him a month to find and capture whoever's making those broadcasts.'

'But you said your boss can find them.'

'My boss can find anything.'

'Then why doesn't he just tell the Empire?'

Vizago threw back his head and laughed. 'The boss working with the Empire? That'll be the day. He'd be happier if they cleared off and were never seen again.' Vizago's smile faltered for a second. 'Although I wouldn't hold your breath.'

The landspeeder turned a corner. They were in the middle of the city now, spires stretching high above them. All around people went about their business, speeder bikes and skimmers dodging each other along the roads.

Everything looked so clean and new, nothing like the slum they'd just come from.

And every now and then, between the towers, Milo caught a glance of the looming Imperial building being built on the other side of town.

'If no-one likes them, why did Lothal invite the Empire here in the first place?' he asked.

'Like we had a choice. Capital City may look good, but the truth of the matter is that the planet was broke. Lothal used to sell crops all over the galaxy, but since the Clone Wars, well, people can't afford to import food any more. All Lothal's customers started growing their own. With no money coming in, the planet was soon in trouble.'

'And the Empire came knocking,' Lina said quietly.

'We welcomed them with open arms, the solution to all our problems.'

They could tell from Vizago's tone that he didn't believe a word he was saying. 'Now they're here, there's no getting rid of them. But hey, Imperial credits are as good as any other. The boss doesn't really mind, as long as the cash keeps coming in.'

'You still haven't said what your boss does,' Lina pointed out.

'You're right, I haven't,' Vizago replied, slowing the landspeeder. 'You can ask him yourself.'

'Why are we stopping here?' Milo asked, as they came to a halt beside a large warehouse.

'Because it's the end of the road.'

Vizago jumped out of the speeder and beamed with pride at a large sign that ran along the side of the building.

'Twin Horns Storage,' he read proudly. 'My *own* little empire.'

'You own a storage company?' Lina asked, hopping out after him.

'Yes and no. Come on.'

The alien marched towards the large front door.

'Can we trust him?' Milo whispered
to his sister as they followed, Morq
clutching his neck.

'No!' insisted CR-8R, although Lina
just shrugged.

'Your guess is as good as mine, but
we haven't exactly got anyone else
to ask.'

Vizago stopped by the door and

waited for them. 'This way please, although the rat will have to stay.'

Milo crossed his arms across his chest. 'Rat?'

'That thing,' said Vizago, pointing at Morq. 'The boss is allergic to monkey-lizards. He uses them for target practice.'

Morq squealed and scampered around Milo's back.

'You better wait here,' Milo said, trying to remove the monkey-lizard from his neck. 'We won't be long, I promise.'

'Allow me,' CR-8R piped up, swinging a manipulator arm towards the animal. Morq snarled and jumped from Milo's back. He landed on the corrugated wall of the building and scampered up to the roof.

'That's better,' said Vizago, leading them through the door. They found themselves in a large reception area, a pair of golden droids sitting behind a front desk. Vizago swaggered towards the robots.

'Got some friends to meet the boss.'

The first robot shook its head, letting out a series of electronic chirps and whistles.

'I don't care if he's not available. He'll want to see these guys, OK?'

The droid continued to argue, but Vizago wasn't having any of it. 'Listen. Either you let me show my friends through, or I test my new blaster on your head.'

To make his point, Vizago's hand dropped down to the holster on his hip.

The two droids whistled at each other, before a door opened behind them.

'Thank you,' Vizago sneered as he stalked past them.

'I thought you said you owned this place?' Milo pointed out, chasing after the alien. 'Shouldn't those two just do what you say?'

Vizago stopped at the doorway. 'Don't ask too many questions, kid. Now, step through the arch.'

Milo did as he was told, a red light washing over him as he passed beneath the archway. Vizago checked a screen set into the wall.

'You're clear. No weapons. Now you, girlie.'

He pointed at Lina who stepped up beside her brother. The red light flashed, although this time was accompanied by a warning bleep. Vizago frowned.

'OK, hands up.'

'What for?' Lina said, although she subconsciously did as she was told. Vizago stalked over to her and grabbed her belt. Flipping open a pouch, he extracted one of the tools that she carried everywhere.

'What's this?' he asked, flicking its activation toggle. A tiny energy blade appeared at the tip.

'Just my fusion torch.'

Vizago regarded her with suspicion. 'Why do you need a cutting tool?'

Milo jumped to his sister's aid. 'You've never travelled in our ship. Lina's always having to fix things.'

Vizago looked Lina up and down, weighing her up. 'Little engineer, eh?'

'I try,' she said, thrusting out her chin.

He pushed the torch back into her hands.

'Keep it in your belt, OK?' he said, walking back to the controls before addressing CR-8R. 'You're next, droid.'

CR-8R hesitated. 'I can assure you I

have nothing to hide.'

Vizago raised a heavy eyebrow. 'It's either the scan, or we dismantle you piece by piece...'

Grumbling, Crater hovered through the door. 'Oh very well.'

Vizago grinned as the screen bleeped again. 'Perfect,' he said, reading the results of the scan. 'Absolutely perfect.'

'Don't tell him that,' Milo muttered beneath his breath. 'His head is big enough as it is!'

'I heard that, Master Milo,' CR-8R complained.

'I think you were supposed to,' Vizago said, winking at Milo. 'Come on.'

He led them into a vast chamber full of stacked crates, each the size of a landspeeder. They stretched all the way up to the ceiling, each crate exactly the same, with grey metal sides and no markings.

'Impressed?' Vizago asked, noting their open mouths.

'There's so many,' Lina said, 'hundreds and hundreds.'

'What's in them?' Milo asked.

Vizago tapped the side of his nose. 'That's for me to know and you to never find out.'

He stepped over to the arch and flipped a switch next to what looked like some kind of alarm button. A shutter slid down, sealing them in.

Beside Lina, CR-8R made an irritated tutting noise. 'Are we supposed to be intimidated, sir?' the droid blurted out. 'You're fooling no-one.'

Vizago regarded the droid with an amused expression. 'Is that so?'

'That security arch is military-grade, far too sophisticated for a two-bit storage company.'

'Oh, we're two-bit now, are we?'

'No,' the droid continued, ignoring Lina's attempts to shut him up. 'You're worse than that. You're a crook. This entire 'business' is obviously just a front for some kind of criminal endeavour.'

Vizago's smile faded. 'And how exactly would you know that?'

The droid wagged a mechanical finger at the alien. 'Your company is as fake as you are, Cikatro Vizago. I just checked the Galactic register. According to the tax records, Twin Horns Storage made little or no profit last year. You want to know what's in the boxes, Master Milo? Nothing but weapons and stolen property, I'd wager. This is a smuggling den!'

'And this is Vilmarh's Revenge,'

snapped Vizago, a blaster suddenly in his hand. It was pointing straight at the droid. 'It's a gift from the boss – an antique, but a powerful one. Keep your vocaliser shut, or I'll blast the head from your shoulders – understand?'

'You can't do this,' said Lina, putting herself between Vizago and the droid.

'Can't I?' the horned alien sneered. 'Yeah, so I don't exactly operate within the law, but guess what? Neither does your mysterious broadcaster. And what about two kids and a droid on the run from the Empire? What does that make them?'

'How do you know the Empire's looking for us?'

The grin returned. 'I didn't – until now. Either way, I wouldn't be too choosy of the company you keep.'

His point made, Vizago slipped his blaster back into its holster and walked over to a control console.

'OK, so I don't know what's in all the boxes,' he admitted, flipping open a panel to reveal a keypad. 'That's the boss's business, but I do know that each crate has its own code. Just punch it in here...'

He tapped a five-digit code with a razor-sharp nail. Above them, one of the crates slid smoothly out of its stack.

'It's got repulsors!' Lina realised.

'They all have,' said Vizago as the crate descended towards them. 'Enter the code and you get your box. Clever, eh?'

The large crate landed softly beside them, its repulsors whirring.

Vizago grinned, before calling out into the warehouse. 'Hey Rom, you there?'

His question was answered by footsteps, as a green-skinned alien appeared from behind the nearest stack. This one was a Rodian with large round eyes and a prominent snout. As he approached, the alien pulled out a stubby blaster which he aimed straight at the children.

'Don't mind Rom,' Vizago said. 'He's just here to keep the contents of this box nice and safe.'

'Safe,' repeated Rom, sluggishly.

'Yeah?' said Milo. 'What's in it?'

'Nothing yet,' replied Vizago, sliding open the crate's door to reveal an empty space inside. 'Get in, now!'

CHAPTER 4

RASK ODAI

'You want us to get in there?' Lina asked, staring into the empty crate.

Vizago chuckled and turned to the Rodian. 'She's a sharp one, eh, Rom?'

The snout-nosed alien echoed Vizago's laugh. 'Yeah, smart!'

'And what if we say no?' Milo asked.

Now Vizago's weapon was back in his palm. 'We're the ones with the blasters, kid! What do you think will happen?'

Milo was fed up with being threatened. Looking behind Vizago and Rom he shouted one word: 'Morq!'

The two aliens turned slightly, expecting to see the monkey-lizard behind them, but it was the distraction Milo needed. He darted around the empty crate, running into the stacks. He had no idea where he was going, or what he would find. Perhaps there was another exit. If he could get out of the warehouse, he could fetch help. Yeah, that was a plan.

He dashed around a nearby stack only to find himself looking at another pile of crates. He turned right, and then left. There were just more crates everywhere, stacked all the way up to the ceiling. It was like being in a maze.

He picked a direction and ran in a straight line, passing column after column of boxes. Then, without warning, a crate slipped out of its stack in front of him. Milo skidded, but couldn't help barging into its side, the clang of the impact echoing around the warehouse.

He pushed himself back the way he'd come, only to find another crate sliding across his path. More crates were hovering into place on both sides too, boxing Milo in. This had to be Vizago, operating them remotely. Milo jumped up, trying to climb the sides of the box in front of him, but the smooth metal was too slippery. He was trapped, with nowhere to go.

'Not bad,' said a voice from above. Milo looked up to see Vizago standing on top of a floating crate. 'You've got spirit. The boss will like that.'

'Didn't get me very far,' Milo grumbled, glaring up at his captor.

'Don't beat yourself up, kid,' Vizago said with a grin. 'We're professionals. It'll take more than a pup like you to get one over on us.'

* * *

Vizago marched Milo back to his sister and CR-8R. Lina threw her arms around him, pulling him close. 'What were you thinking, Milo? They could have blasted you!'

He knew it had been stupid, but he'd had to try – not that it had done them any good. Rom herded them all into the crate, following them through the open door, his blaster never wavering. Milo covered his nose. The inside of the crate reeked of rotten fish.

'Enjoy your trip,' said Vizago from outside.

'Wait,' pleaded Lina. 'What are you going to do with us?'

Smirking, Vizago pressed a button on the side of the box and the door slid shut, plunging them into darkness. Milo ran forward and banged on the closed door.

'Let us out of here! Let us out!'

Lights flickered into life on the ceiling, illuminating the claustrophobic box.

'Away from the door,' Rom grunted, as the crate lurched, its repulsors powering up with a whine.

Outside, they could hear the keypad beep as Vizago entered a longer, eight-digit code.

'We're moving,' said CR-8R, sweeping forward to catch Milo who stumbled with the sudden movement.

Milo steadied himself. It felt like they were flying up into the air.

'You can't keep us in here,' Lina told Rom. 'We have friends who know we're here,' she lied. 'Big friends. With bigger blasters than yours.'

'I like blasters,' commented Rom, blankly.

Lina joined her brother and the droid, Rom's barrel following her.

'Crater,' she whispered. 'Can you burn your way out of this?'

CR-8R turned to look at the walls of the crate. 'I don't know. That looks like duramentium, one of the toughest steels in the galaxy.'

Lina sighed. 'Which means my fusion torch will be next to useless too.'

CR-8R nodded. 'Unfortunately that warty thug would blast us before we could even make a dent.'

'Rom blasts fast,' the Rodian commented. Milo sighed. There was obviously nothing wrong with Rom's ears.

The box shifted beneath their feet, changing direction.

Lina turned to the Rodian. 'Where are you taking us?'

'Yeah,' said Milo. 'And why did

Vizago trap you in here too?'

Rom didn't answer.

'Can you understand me?' Milo said, speaking louder and slower. 'Why. Are. You. Here?'

'Rom not trapped,' the alien replied. 'You not trapped either.'

'Well, it certainly looks that way to me,' commented CR-8R, before a sudden jolt caused him to dip slightly on his repulsors. Milo fell back into Lina, who slipped her hand into his. They'd stopped moving.

'Now what?' Lina asked.

'Now you meet boss,' Rom informed her as the door slid open to reveal a long narrow room beyond. Without another word, the Rodian stepped out of the crate and onto thick carpet.

'I assume we're supposed to follow,' CR-8R said, as they did exactly that.

The room had been constructed

from four or five crates bolted together. It had the same lights in the ceiling, although the smooth walls were lined with exotic works of art, paintings of seascapes and underwater worlds. At the far end was a beautifully carved desk with a high-backed chair. Above the desk, half a dozen hovering platforms buzzed in the air like insects. Each held treasures of a bygone age. Giant crystals, an ornate metal box, an armoured gauntlet. However, Milo's eyes were fixed on the hulking figure that stood behind the desk.

'Oh my,' CR-8R said out loud, his synthetic voice quivering. 'An IG assassin droid.'

'Yes, Crater,' Lina said, trying to shut him up.

'You don't understand, Miss Lina,' CR-8R continued regardless. 'Assassin droids are incredibly dangerous.

They're walking armouries, complete
with integrated concussion grenade
launchers and flame-throwers.'

'Yes, Crater. Enough now.'

'Although I've always been quite
jealous of their acid-proof servo wires.
I've always wanted some of th–'

'Crater, shut up!' Lina snapped.

'Droid talks a lot,' said Rom,
stopping beside the table.

'You're telling us,' replied Milo, before turning his attention to the assassin droid. 'Are you the boss?'

'No, he is not!' burbled a voice from hidden speakers. Milo looked around to see where it was coming from.

'Who said that?'

'Is IG-70 the boss, indeed?' the voice continued, as a panel opened in one of the walls. Milo gasped. Beyond the wall was a tank of yellow, briny water, held back by a force field. Swimming in the murky liquid was an imposing figure, with large bulbous eyes on the side of a high-domed head. Milo immediately recognised the alien as a native of Mon Cala. The *Whisper Bird* had visited the watery planet when Milo was small, their dad having made many friends among the Mon Calamari when he'd first started exploring the Outer Rim.

This one looked anything but

friendly.

'Boss,' Rom told them helpfully, as the alien swam through the energy barrier that kept the water from flooding the room. Dripping all over the expensive carpet, the Mon Calamari slopped over to the desk to sit down with a squelch on the chair.

'Boss have good bath?' Rom asked.

'No, I did not,' the alien replied testily. 'The water's stale. Recycle it, will you?'

Rom did as he was told, pressing a control beside the side of the tank. Behind the force field, the murky liquid drained away to be replaced by much cleaner water.

'Now,' the Mon Calamari said, sniffing the air. 'Who are you? And why do you smell of monkey-lizards?'

'Who are we?' Milo repeated, sounding braver than he felt. 'Who are *you*?'

The alien's nostrils flared and he turned to Rom. 'This is why I don't like children,' he gurgled. 'Impertinent sea-slugs.'

'Sea-slugs,' Rom repeated, sounding like he hadn't understood a word that his boss had just said.

The Mon Calamari leant forward, water pooling around his elbows. 'I am Rask Odai, and this is my planet.'

'I thought it was the Empire's planet,' Lina pointed out.

'That's what I let them believe.' He waved a webbed hand as if dismissing an annoying servant. 'Oh, they can worry about *governing*, and *law* and *order*. That's all too boring for me. I'm more interested in the important things in life.' He grinned, revealing toothless gums. 'Like money!'

All the time, Odai's goggle-like eyes were focused on CR-8R. As Milo watched, the Mon Calamari licked his blubbery lips. He shuddered. Did this fishy freak eat droids or something?

His watery eyes still locked onto the droid, Odai asked them what they wanted.

'Didn't Vizago let you know why we're here?' Lina asked.

'If he did, I wouldn't have to ask!' Odai snapped, his voice rising.

'S-sorry,' Lina said, raising her hands apologetically. She told the gangster why they'd come to Lothal, how they were looking for the source of the rebel transmissions.

'Is that all?' Odai replied, scratching the long fronds that dangled from his bottom lip. 'That's easy.'

'Easy,' repeated Rom.

Odai opened a drawer in his desk and pulled out a handheld device.

'I don't suppose either of you

understand communication frequencies?' the crime lord gurgled.

'Lina does,' Milo chipped in. 'She's brilliant with machines.'

'Is she now?' Odai said, beckoning her with a webbed finger.

Lina cautiously stepped closer, under the ever-watchful gaze of the assassin droid.

Odai started working the scanner, static bursting out of its tinny speakers. Lina walked around the table to see what the Mon Calamari was doing. At the twist of a dial, a voice broke through the static – cultured and cold.

'All troops report to barracks. Training will commence at–'

Odai turned another control and the voice dissolved again. 'We use these to eavesdrop on our Imperial neighbours,' he explained. 'Just in case they're

doing anything interesting. Now, if
you take a scanner like this and use
it to search for background chatter,
channels that only droids use for
communication...'

Another voice broke through, but it
wasn't an Imperial message this time.

*'We'll be back on the airwaves later
today,'* it said. *'In the meantime, stand
up for what you believe, not what the
Emperor tells you to think. You were
born free. Hold onto that. Treasure it.'*

'That's him,' Milo said, excitedly.
'That's the transmission!'

Odai pressed a couple of buttons,
showing Lina each step of the process.
'Get the scanner to lock onto the signal
and you should be able to track it, see?
Like a detector.' The device started
to beep rhythmically. 'The nearer you
get to the source of the broadcast, the
louder the beep.'

'That's brilliant,' Lina admitted.

Odai slammed the scanner down onto the top of the table. 'I know. Now, about my payment...'

'Payment?' she said, glancing nervously at Milo. 'Vizago never said anything about payment.'

'What do you think I am, a charity?' Odai sneered. 'I gave you what you want, now you give me something.'

'But we don't have any money,' Milo tried to argue. 'Not much anyway.'

'I don't want your credits.'

'Then what do you want?' Lina asked.

Odai turned to the assassin droid. 'IG-70?'

The droid nodded. 'Understood.'

Without another word, the tall droid marched from the back of the room, heading straight for Milo and CR-8R.

'What's he going to do?' Lina asked the Mon Calamari.

'Collect my payment,' Odai replied, rubbing his webbed fingers together.

'Keep back,' CR-8R warned, putting himself in front of Milo. 'I won't let you hurt these children.'

'Understood,' repeated IG-70 as he reached up with a large pincer and grabbed CR-8R's metal face.

With an electronic grunt, the assassin droid ripped CR-8R's head clean from his shoulders.

CHAPTER 5

THE MOVEABLE FEAST

'What are you doing?' cried Milo as sparks burst from CR-8R's neck. The headless droid's arms dropped lifelessly to his side as IG-70 marched its prize back towards Odai.

Milo sprung forward, trying to grab CR-8R's head, but was swatted aside easily by the giant assassin droid.

'Give it to me,' Odai gurgled, his arms outstretched. He snatched the head from IG-70's hands and turned it over in his fingers. 'Yes, yes. This is perfect. Absolutely perfect.'

'Give that back,' Lina said, making a lunge for the head, only to find IG-70's blaster swinging around to point at her.

'Information: you will freeze,' the droid rumbled.

Begrudgingly, Lina raised her hands and took a step back.

'But what do you want with Crater's head?' Milo asked from the floor.

'You're kidding, right?' the Mon Calamari said, his pink tongue wetting those horribly blubbery lips. 'This is a genuine architect droid head. A Mark IV. I haven't seen one for decades.'

'What if it is?' asked Lina. 'It belongs to CR-8R, not you!'

'It's payment for services provided,' Odai snapped back. 'You have your transmission; I have the droid's head. Fair and square.'

'But it can't be worth anything to you!'

'Not worth anything? This will be the jewel in my collection.' He threw out his other arm, indicating the treasures on the floating platforms. 'It will have pride of place.'

'Among that junk?' Milo sneered.

'Junk? This isn't junk? I have the finest collection of Old Republic artefacts this side of Nar Shaddaa. This head was wasted on your droid. It's an antique.'

He opened another drawer in his desk and pulled out a hover-platform. Standing CR-8R's head on a plinth, he ran a webbed finger around the platform and gurgled with pleasure as it floated out of his hands to join the rest of his collection.

'No,' shouted Milo, jumping up towards the desk. 'You can't just go around stealing people's heads.'

An arm snaked around his neck, pulling him back as a blaster pressed hard against his head. It was Rom, the

Rodian hissing in Milo's ear.

'Boss can do anything he wants.'

'Besides,' added Odai, admiring his latest acquisition, 'I didn't steal anything. It was a legitimate trade. Now get these two sea-slugs out of my sight!'

* * *

On the streets of Lothal, a figure in a long cloak swept back and forth on a speeder bike.

As he scanned the streets, the wrist-mounted comlink on his arm buzzed. The man raised the device to his hooded face.

'*Have you found them?*' a voice asked over the comms-signal.

'Not yet,' he replied. 'Are we sure they're even here.'

Before his contact could reply, a landspeeder roared up along the road. The man backed his bike into an alleyway to observe the newcomer slow to a stop.

The craft was piloted by a Devaronian, the horned alien flanked by a Rodian and an old assassin droid. As the man watched, the two aliens threw a boy and a girl from the back of the speeder. The children landed in a pile in the dirt as the Rodian manhandled

a heap of broken machinery from the floating vehicle. No, it wasn't just any old machinery – it was a droid, minus its head by the look of things. It bobbed lifelessly on its repulsors.

'Please,' the girl was saying, 'don't do this!'

'You going to stop us?' the Devaronian laughed as the headless droid was pushed from the speeder. 'Now do yourself a favour, kid. Don't come back!'

With that, the three rogues zoomed off, leaving the children lying in the road.

The man spoke into his comlink. 'Do you see them?'

'*Yes,*' came the tinny reply.

'Shall I bring them in?'

'*Not yet,*' the voice told him. '*We need to be sure...*'

* * *

It was a long walk back to the landing
strip. By the time they'd reached the
shanty town, Milo and Lina's feet were
aching and their hearts were heavy.
They had started the journey talking
animatedly about what they would do
to Rask Odai when they saw him again,

imagining all kinds of revenge, but the reality was that it was hopeless.

'Even if we could get past the security arch,' Lina said, carrying CR-8R's floating body on her back, 'we'd never be able to find his office again, not without knowing what code to enter into the crate controls.'

'And then there's Rom and that droid,' Milo added. 'You think they'll just let us take Crater's head?'

The *Whisper Bird* was in front of them as they trudged across the muddy port. 'We'll think of something,' Lina promised him. 'There'll be something on board the *Bird* that can help. You'll see!'

But Milo's eyes had gone wide. 'Morq! I forgot about Morq!' He looked around, panicked by the sudden realisation. 'He must still be back at Twin Horns Storage!'

'Maybe he came back to the *Bird*?'
Lina suggested, but Milo was already
off, half slipping on the mud as he raced
for the ship. He ran around the *Whisper
Bird*, calling the monkey-lizard's name,
becoming increasingly frantic with
every shout.

'Morq! Morq!'

Leaving CR-8R's body behind, Lina
ran up to him. 'Milo, keep it down.
People are looking!'

'He's not here, Lina,' Milo said. 'He's
back in the city. He'll be so scared. He's
all alone.'

And with that Milo's face crumpled
as tears started to flow. Lina couldn't
move quick enough to stop her brother
collapsing to his knees in the mud, his
face in his hands.

She dropped down beside him,
throwing her arms around him, pulling
him close.

'There, there,' she said, her own voice catching as she realised that it was usually their mum who said those words. 'It's going to be OK.'

'No it's not,' he cried out, sobs wracking his body. 'Morq's gone. Crater's gone. Mum and Dad are gone. And there's nothing we can do about it.'

'Of course there is,' Lina told him, although she wasn't sure she believed it herself. Sitting here, in the shadow of the *Whisper Bird* on a strange planet with no friends. The tears that ran down her own face were long overdue. Both of them had gone through so much, and they were still no nearer finding their parents. It seemed like the entire galaxy was against them. If it wasn't the Empire, it was monsters and if it wasn't monsters it was gangsters like Odai.

As she sat cradling her weeping

brother, Lina had finally run out
of ideas. Sure there were the
transmissions, but even if what Odai
had told them was true, how did they
know they could trust whoever was
making the broadcasts?

How could they trust anyone
anymore?

'Looks like someone needs a good
lunch!'

Lina looked up, her arms still around
Milo. A woman was standing in front
of them, her hands on her hips. She had
a kind, open face, with dark skin and
bright green eyes. Her hair was bunched
into tight curls, held in place with a
bright orange band, and she wore a long
knitted shawl over an apron and a pair
of well-worn overalls.

'Unless you're not hungry.' She
added, when neither of them replied.

'I am,' Milo said meekly, wiping the

back of his hand across his nose.

Lina smiled, even when breaking his heart her brother thought with his stomach. 'It has been a while since we ate anything.'

'Then what are you waiting for?' said the woman. 'Follow me.'

Nervously, Milo got to his feet, wiping tears away on his sleeve. Together, they walked hand in hand, following the woman around the *Whisper Bird*.

There, parked in the next bay, was another ship, one that hadn't been there before. It was an old freighter – a *very* old freighter, the kind Lina's mum had shown her in old holo-reels. It looked like it had seen a lot of action, its dented hull pitted with years of asteroid strikes. That wasn't the strangest thing about it though. One of the cargo doors was open, revealing what looked like a

small kitchen and counter. Metal tables
were dotted around the opening, each
occupied by the same alien wretches
that had watched the children's arrival
which such suspicion. Now, they
were tucking into warm meals eaten
off metal plates. Lina breathed in. It
all smelled so good. Soups, stews and
freshly baked bread. Her stomach
gurgled. She was hungry too. She hadn't
realised how much.

'That's it, that's it,' said the woman, beckoning them forward. 'Welcome to the *Moveable Feast*. Yes, there are prettier ships out there, faster ships even, but none that serve the food of Captain Shalla Mondatha. Here, take a seat.'

She pulled out a stool from beneath a free table, producing a cloth from her pocket to wipe the metal surface free of crumbs.

'Captain who?' Milo asked, slipping onto the stool.

'Shalla Mondatha,' the woman repeated. 'You must have heard the name?'

'I'm afraid not,' admitted Lina, joining her brother.

'Well, you have now,' beamed the woman. 'You're looking at her. Captain, cook and chief bottle-washer. Pleased to meet you.'

Nearby, on another table, there was

a clatter of plates. Lina turned to see a chubby Dowutin attempting to stop a small scavenger from helping itself to his lunch. In trying to swat the creature away, the orange-skinned alien had only succeeded in knocking over his table.

'Hey,' Shalla shouted out. 'Watch what you're doing!'

'It's this thing,' the Dowutin complained, pointing behind the overturned table. 'It was stealing my food.'

There was an angry squeak, and Milo jumped up from his stool. 'Wait! That's–'

At the sound of Milo's voice, Morq leapt up on the capsized table. The monkey-lizard let out a squeal of delight, before racing over to jump into Milo's arms. Lina's brother hugged his pet, who chirruped happily as he licked Milo's face.

'Someone's pleased to see you,' Shalla laughed.

'Morq! I thought I'd lost you! But you came back! Of course you did, you clever boy!'

'What about my food?' the Dowutin complained.

'By the size of that belly, it looks like you've had enough,' Shalla shouted back. 'Off with you. I've got hungry mouths to feed.'

Turning her attention back to the children, Shalla pulled a datapad from her apron pocket. 'Now what can I get for you. Today's specials are Melahnese red curry, Melahnese green curry and Melahnese yellow curry.'

'Do you have anything that isn't Melahnese curry?' Milo asked.

'Of course I do,' Shalla laughed, her eyes sparkling. 'I can do you nerf pie, berbersian crab salad, bhudde and orxtle stew...'

'Nerf pie please,' Milo said, his earlier tears forgotten.

Shalla smiled and turned to Lina. 'And for you, dear?'

'The salad, please.'

'Do you want dindra sauce with that?'

Lina licked her lips. She hadn't tasted dindra in years.

'Yes please!'

Shalla gave the children another dazzling smile and slipped the datapad into her apron pocket. 'You got it!'

She disappeared into the *Feast*, only to reappear minutes later with two plates laden with food.

Milo gazed at the giant slab of pie as it was placed in front of him. 'That looks amazing!'

Lina's salad looked just as inviting. 'It does, but how much will it cost?' She looked up at the Captain, biting her lip. 'We haven't got a lot of credits.'

Shalla leant close to them and whispered: 'It's on the house. Just don't tell everyone. They'll all be wanting freebies!'

She pulled up a stool of her own and sat at the table. 'What are you waiting for? Dive in!'

The children didn't need telling twice. Grabbing cutlery from a metal tub, they set about their meals, cramming forkfuls of the gorgeous food into their mouths. Lina let out a groan of appreciation. It tasted so good. The Naboo lettuce was crisp and fresh, while the buttered crab sticks melted on her tongue. And as for the sauce! It was so tangy that that her taste buds felt like they were dancing!

'Good?' Shalla enquired.

'*Moh yefph!*' Milo enthused with his

mouth full, gravy running down his chin.

Shalla laughed. 'You know, I travel this entire sector, setting up shop from port to port. I've cooked for freighter crews all along the Kessel Run and I've never seen anyone enjoy my food as much as you two!'

'It's really good,' Lina said, taking another bite.

Shalla smiled fondly, and for a moment a deep sadness seemed to shadow her usually cheerful features. 'You remind me of my own daughter.'

'Does she travel with you?' asked Milo.

'Mercy me, no,' Shalla replied, regaining her composure. 'She's all grown up now. Off having adventures of her own – but it's good to feed you two. Don't see a lot of kids in places like this, and for good reason.'

She placed a kind hand on Lina's arm. 'What are you doing here, honey?'

Perhaps it was the food in their bellies, or the warmth of Shalla's smile, but the children told her everything. About their parents, about Captain Korda, about coming to Lothal and losing CR-8R's head.

'They just ripped it from his shoulders?' Shalla asked in amazement as they finished their story.

Suddenly, Lina felt the pang of loss again. 'And we need it back. Crater's one of the most annoying droids you've ever met. He's stubborn and argumentative and so, so superior, but–'

'But he's yours,' Shalla said softly.

Lina nodded. 'He's all we've got left.'

'Plus these maps your mum left you...'

'Are in his head,' Milo told Shalla.

'Well, that settles it. First, I'm going

to get you both a bowl of Bosphian trifle and then we're going to make plans.'

Milo frowned, wiping a crumb of pastry from his lips. 'Plans for what?'

Shalla smiled slyly. 'Oh, I wasn't always a cook, Milo Graf. Long ago, in another life, I used to be a *smuggler*.'

Lina felt her eyes go wide as Shalla continued.

'I've picked up a few tricks over the years. This Odai guy stole your droid's head? Well, we're going to steal it right back!'

CHAPTER 6

BEETLES

Later that day, as Lothal's sun began to dip in the sky, Shalla Mondatha zoomed up to the entrance of Twin Horns Storage on a shiny silver speeder bike. She still wore her old knitted shawl, but the apron was gone and a wrap-around visor covered her eyes. Behind her speeder bumped a medium-sized container, hovering on a repulsor-bed. She peered through the open doors, watching Cikatro Vizago's goons lugging crates around the lobby. Her eyes narrowed behind her glasses as she watched a Rodian slink down the street and in through the doors.

That must be Rom, she thought, recalling what the children had told her. It was now or never.

Leaping from the bike, she uncoupled the crate and pushed it into the warehouse.

'Hey,' said Vizago, stepping in front of her. 'Where are you going with that?'

Shalla narrowed her eyes. 'What do you mean?'

The Devaronian tapped her crate. 'What I said! Where are you going with this container?'

Shalla shrugged. 'It's to go in my crate.' She looked around herself, feigning ignorance. 'This is Twin Corn Storage, isn't it?'

'Twin *Horns*,' Vizago corrected her. 'A private business.'

She gave him one of her biggest smiles. 'Then I'm in the right place. I had my droid open an account earlier today. I need somewhere safe to store my ingredients when I'm off-world.' When he didn't comment, Shalla added her name helpfully. 'Captain Shalla Mondatha.'

Vizago glanced at one of the two golden droids behind the main counter. It was already checking the Twin

Horn's customer lists. Finding a name on the screen, the droid burbled a reply at Vizago.

The Devaronian turned back towards her, an insincere smile on his lips. 'My mistake. I understand you paid for our premium service.'

Shalla nodded enthusiastically. 'Oh yes. Only the best for my food.'

'We're going to have to scan your crate,' said Vizago. 'Nothing personal, you understand. Just standard procedure.'

'Of course. That's why I chose your establishment. *Security is our business,* isn't that what your brochure said?'

Vizago humoured her with another smile before turning to the Rodian. 'Rom, scan the crate.'

The Rodian looked confused. 'But Rom see boss?'

'You can see him *after* you've

scanned the crate,' Vizago insisted.

Grumbling, Rom grabbed a handheld scanner and waved it over the container. Immediately, the scanner beeped furiously.

'Picked up life-sign!' Rom reported.

Vizago's smile faded. 'Open it up.'

Shalla shook her head. 'I-I can't do that.'

'Then it can't stay here.'

'You don't understand!'

'Then *show* me.'

Shalla sighed, letting her shoulders sag. 'Very well. It looks like I have little choice.'

'No,' Vizago agreed. 'You don't.'

Shalla ran her hand along the side of the container until she found a control. She pressed the button and the lid split in two, opening on hinges that squeaked noisily.

Rainbow-coloured beetles swarmed

from the open container, spilling onto the floor. The Devaronian jumped back.

'Ugh! What are they?'

'Wakizan beetles,' Shalla said, watching the insects scurry everywhere. 'They're quite the delicacy in the Core Worlds. I fry them in troogan oil.' She fished a paper bag out of her pocket, offering it to the disgusted Devaronian. 'Would you like to try one?'

'No I wouldn't!' Vizago insisted, so Shalla tried Rom instead. The Rodian took a beetle gladly, popping it into his snout and crunching loudly.

'Rom like!' he announced, and so Shalla gave him another. Step one of the plan was in progress.

Step two happened as a red-furred creature scampered into the lobby, making a beeline for the beetles. It was Morq, chattering happily at the

free meal.

'And now the monkey-runt is back,' shouted Vizago. 'Today just gets better. Shut the lid. Shut the lid!'

'Yes, of course,' said Shalla, fiddling with the control, and pretending that it wasn't working. 'Oh, I think it's stuck.'

All the time, Morq jumped around excitedly, and the insects scurried everywhere at once.

'Can Rom see boss now?' Rom asked.

'Yes,' Vizago snapped. 'Go! There'll be one less pest here!'

Rom sloped off, stepping through the security arch and operating the control pad at the front of the warehouse with sticky fingers. Shalla watched as a crate started floating towards him, presumably to take the Rodian to Odai.

Finally, she pressed the lid closed, cutting off the flow of beetles.

'I'm ever so sorry,' Shalla said as an excited Morq leapt up onto Vizago's head to swing off the alien's horns. 'But if we hadn't have opened the container...'

'Yes, yes,' barked Vizago, trying to grab the monkey-lizard. Shalla used the distraction to glance again at the warehouse. Rom was gone now, spirited away in a crate, but she was staring at the keypad he'd used, the hidden camera in her visor taking a picture.

She pulled out a small metal tin and started to scatter tiny pellets on the floor. Morq jumped down, popped one into his mouth before spitting it back out in disgust and darting back out towards the street.

'Now what are you doing?' moaned Vizago.

'It's beetle food. They won't be able to resist, see?' Sure enough, the insects started scurrying towards her, following the trail of pellets. 'I can't cook with this lot now, but I can get rid of them for you. Will you deliver my container into storage?'

'Yes, yes. If you clear my lobby, I'll deliver it anyway you want.'

Shalla grinned. 'Thank you! I look

forward to doing more business with you.'

Before Vizago could cancel her account, Shalla hurried out of the building, the hungry beetles scuttling after her. When they were far enough away from the front doors, she threw the tin to the side where it clattered against a wall. Pellets spilled everywhere, the beetles descending on them like a swarm.

The doors of Twin Horns Storage swung shut. Shalla returned to her speeder bike, to find Morq waiting for her on the saddle. She gave the monkey-lizard a friendly tickle under the chin. 'Good work fella. That went better than I'd hoped.'

She pressed a hidden button on the side of her visor and viewed the image she had taken of the keypad. '*Much* better.'

The press of another button transmitted the picture to a second pair of glasses inside the building. Nudging Morq out of the way, she threw her leg over the speeder bike and started the engine.

The heist was on!

CHAPTER 7

FIRE ALARM

In Twin Horns Storage, Cikatro Vizago crushed a lone beetle under his boot.

'Bugs,' he complained, lifting his foot to see the gloopy mess on the floor. 'I hate them.'

'What should we do with this thing?' said one of his lackeys, a trunk-nosed Onodone who wore a patch over one of his jet-black eyes.

Vizago looked at the container and sighed. 'She's paid her money, so we better look after it. I've got a feeling that Captain Mondatha is the kind of woman who would run to the authorities if we lost her stock. But wait...'

The Devaronian walked over to a side desk, returning with two lengths of rod. He held them over the container and they jumped from his hand to land onto the lid with a clang, gripping the container like a pair of long limpets.

'Gravity seals,' he explained to the puzzled Onodone. 'Just in case any of those insects try to push open the lid. Nothing can get out of it now.'

* * *

Inside the container, something – or rather some*one* – *desperately* wanted to get out. Beneath the pile of squirming beetles lay Lina, curled in a ball with her brother beside her.

Both of them wore black jumpsuits and gloves that Shalla had provided, promising that the beetles wouldn't be able to burrow in through the seams.

Visor-like glasses protected their eyes, and breathing masks were clamped over their mouths.

Lina had her arms wrapped tightly around her head, her eyes screwed tight behind the visor. This was the worst thing she'd ever had to do. The beetles were everywhere, pressed up against her skin and wriggling through her hair.

The bugs were packed in so tightly that they could barely move, but their little legs scratched against her. Then there was the noise – hundreds of tiny jaws clicking together as one.

She wanted to scream and shout and brush the horrible creatures from her skin, but knew she had to wait.

The container was moving again, swaying as it was pushed deeper into the warehouse. She'd heard Vizago's muffled command through the constant chatter of the insects.

'Take it to the holding area for processing. We'll deal with it later.'

Just as Shalla had said – they would leave the container alone, long enough for them to escape. Even so, Lina could feel herself panic. What if the plan didn't work? What if Shalla's beetles were put straight into a storage crate? They'd be trapped until someone opened the box again. Or worse, they'd be left there, in the darkness, with only insects for company.

Lina forced herself to calm down. They'd worked it all out. Shalla had told them exactly what to do. Lina just had to be patient.

The container thudded as it was lowered to the floor, scaring the already squirming beetles. Lina listened until she heard the footsteps slope away.

Count to ten, she told herself, *maybe twenty. Make sure there's no-one around.*

Everything was silent, save for the chittering of the insects. The container had been left in the processing area.

'Milo,' she hissed through her breathing mask. 'We need to move!'

Her brother shifted beside her, pushing up through the beetles to shove against the lid of the container.

'It's not budging...' he said, grunting

with the effort. 'Those gravity seals must be holding it tight.'

Lina shifted around, planting her feet against the side of the container. 'Shalla said there's a loose panel over here, just in case we got stacked with something heavy on top.'

She pushed with her feet. Nothing happened.

'It's stuck. Help me, will you?'

Milo joined her, pushing against the side with his own feet. Still nothing.

'Why isn't it moving?' Lina started to kick, not caring if anyone heard her. She had to get out of here.

'Lina, calm down,' urged Milo. 'We can do this. We just need to work together.'

'No,' she said, kicking with every word. 'Need. To. Get. Out. Now.'

With the last kick, the loose panel came free and clattered on the floor. The beetles streamed out like a wave, Lina wriggling her way through the gap. As soon as she was out of the container, she jumped to her feet, brushing the last remaining beetles from her.

Milo slid out beside her. 'Keep it down, will you!'

She froze. He was right. Had anyone heard?

As the beetles scampered to freedom, the children stood, listening. There were no shouts, no running footsteps.

They'd done it.

Pulling her breathing mask down, Lina ran to the corner of a stack of crates and peered around. They were alone in the warehouse, for now at least.

She glanced along the wall, spotting a red button behind protective glass. An alarm, like the one by the arch. She nodded at Milo who, keeping his head down, raced across to the wall. Turning his head away, he smashed the glass and pressed the button. The alarm sounded immediately, an ear-splitting wail that echoed around the warehouse. Milo scampered back as they heard people running for the exit. Then, a whine from above told them that a crate was descending. It landed in front of the security arch and the door slid open. Lina watched as Rask Odai exited the crate, flanked by Rom and IG-70, who hurried their complaining boss out of the warehouse.

Lina waited for the main doors to close before grabbing Milo's arm and pulling him towards the waiting crate. They reached the keypad and Lina pressed a button on the side of her visor. An image appeared on the back of the lens. It was the picture Shalla had taken using a special filter that highlighted Rom's oil-covered fingerprints on the buttons. If Lina worked back from the faintest print to the oiliest, she'd be able to work out the code that would take them to Odai's office.

Well, that was the theory anyway.

Milo was already in the crate. 'Come on!'

'I'm going as fast as I can,' she said, following the fingerprints to type out the code. The keypad beeped as Lina completed the sequence and she jumped through the door just as it began to close.

Inside the crate, the lights flickered on, and they began to rise, the repulsors lifting them high into the air. This time it seemed to take even longer than their first trip.

'Do you think they've worked out there's no fire yet?' Lina asked, tapping her foot against the crate floor.

'I hope not,' Milo replied as the crate clanked into place.

The door slid open to reveal Odai's office. So far so good! The children ran towards the ornate desk.

'There it is,' shouted Milo, pointing at CR-8R's head floating on its platform. 'It's high up!'

Milo grabbed Odai's chair, and pulled it beneath the hovering plinth. 'Hold this steady.'

As he clambered onto the chair, the klaxon stopped screeching.

'That's the end of the fire alarm,' Milo said.

'Then they'll be coming back. Hurry up.'

'OK!' Milo said, stretching up to the platform. It was still too high, his fingers barely reaching the plinth.

'Let me,' Lina told him. 'I'm taller.'

'I can do it,' Milo insisted, standing on tiptoes to grab the edge of the platform. Beneath him, the chair flipped over

and he fell, knocking the platform as
he tumbled to the floor. CR-8R's head
rocked, before toppling over the edge to
land on Milo's back.

There was no time to celebrate. A new
siren cut through the air, shriller than
even the fire alarm.

'*Warning!*' boomed a computerised voice. '*Robbery in progress! Warning! Robbery in progress!*'

Lina grabbed CR-8R's head and helped Milo to his feet. 'I think we just lost the element of surprise!'

CHAPTER 8

FEELING FLUSHED

At the far end of the office, the children's crate dropped away and Lina ran to look down at the rapidly descending box. 'This is your fault. If you'd let *me* get Crater's head, we would never have set off the alarm.'

Milo joined her at the edge of the room. 'My fault? You were supposed to be holding the chair!' He peered at the warehouse floor far below. 'We're a long way up, aren't we?'

'I guess Odai likes looking down at his kingdom.'

'Yeah, talking about Odai...' Milo said, pointing at another crate that was rising towards them. This one's door was already open, the Mon Calamari standing in the gap. Rom and IG-70 were beside him, their blasters raised.

'They don't look happy to see us,' said Milo as the first shots hammered against the outside of the office.

'What are we going to do?' asked Lina, jumping back from the opening. She looked around the office in desperation. 'That's the only way out.'

Milo's hand went to the breathing mask around his neck. 'No, it's not. When did we last have a bath?'

Lina stared at the tank of water set into the wall. 'You're joking!'

Milo ran back to the floating platforms and hopped up onto the desk to grab a large silver box from one of the plinths.

'That should do it,' he said, jumping back down to the carpet.

'Do what?'

Milo opened the box's lid and ran back to Lina. 'I don't know if CR-8R's head is waterproof.'

'You're not joking,' Lina groaned, slipping the droid's head inside the box. Milo snapped the lid shut.

'Nope. You first.'

'Why me?'

The whine of the approaching crate was getting louder with every second.

'OK,' Milo conceded. 'I'll lead the way, if you're scared.'

Lina gave him her best withering look as he popped his breathing mask over his mouth and hurried to the force field. Taking a deep breath, he pushed his hand through the energy barrier, pulling his hand back out as soon as it got wet.

'It's freezing!'

'Changing your mind?'

An energy bolt shot through the open

door to slam against the ceiling.

'Not on your life,' Milo said, jumping through the force field. Lina ran to the controls and tried to remember how Rom had operated the flush.

'Directive: stop where you are!' came a shout from the open door. The crate was almost in place, IG-70's blaster pointing right at her. 'Drop the head!'

'No, don't!' yelled Odai. 'You'll break it! Just stay where you are!'

'Sorry, can't do that,' Lina shouted back. 'See you!'

She slammed her palm down on the control and the water whooshed from the tank, taking Milo with it. Clutching the metal box to her chest, Lina dived into the force field. She had the vague impression of two blaster bolts passing behind her back before she plunged into the icy water.

It was like jumping into a whirlpool.

One second she was in the tank and then she had been sucked down a pipe, bashing against its slimy sides as she was pushed along with the current. She called out for Milo, but there was no answer. All she could do was hold onto the box and hope for the best.

Her head bashed against the side of the pipe, knocking her visor from her face. Salty water stung her eyes as she

looked around, trying to see her brother.

And then she found him – by slamming hard against his body!

He cried out as the remainder of the water washed past them, out through the circular grate that Milo had crashed into.

'Are you OK?' she asked, pulling her breathing mask aside.

Milo was pushing against the grille. 'This thing won't budge.'

She put the silver box to the side and joined in, heaving against the heavy metal grate. The stink coming from the other side told her that they were probably down in Lothal's sewer system, but as long as they were nowhere near Odai and his goons, she didn't care.

'It's no good,' she said, wiggling her fingers through the holes on the grille. 'There must be some kind of lock.'

She worked her way around the edge

of the grating, finally finding a block of cold steel jutting out.

'That's got to be it. Look after Crater's head.'

Milo picked up the silver box, as Lina reached for the tools in her belt.

'What are you going to do?' he asked.

Lina pulled her fusion torch out of its pouch. 'Maybe nothing if this got too wet.'

She pressed the button on the edge of the small metal cylinder, but nothing happened. She gave it a shake and tried again. This time a tiny red energy blade lanced forward.

'Can I borrow your visor?'

Milo passed his glasses to her. Covering her eyes, she plunged the tip of the cutter into the grille on the other side of the lock. Sparks rained down on her as she sliced through the metal, acrid smoke filling the pipe. Pushing her breathing mask over her mouth, she slid the torch across the back of the lock and, with a crash, the grille clattered open.

Lina slipped the torch back into her belt and jumped down onto a small ledge that ran along the side of the sewer.

'Here, take this,' Milo said, passing the silver box down to her before scrambling out of the pipe himself. Fading sunlight was streaming through grilles in the ceiling high above. The sun was going down. They needed to move. It wouldn't be long before IG-70 and Rom came running.

'There's some steps,' said Milo, edging his way along the ledge towards a ladder set into the brickwork. Lina followed, careful not to drop the silver box. She just hoped that Shalla was waiting for them, up on the street.

* * *

Outside Twin Horns Storage, Shalla
sat back on her speeder bike, stroking
Morq's head. Something was wrong. The
plan had been clear; set off the alarm and
while everyone was outside, grab the
droid's head. Then the children were to
return to the container and hide again.
Shalla would bluster into the reception,
making a fuss that there had been
an alarm and demanding her beetles
immediately. She'd walk out with the
children safely back beneath the bugs.
Simple.

But a second alarm had sent Odai
and his henchmen scuttling back into
the building. Had the children been
discovered?

Morq let out a worried squeal, as
the Mon Calamari reappeared out of
the warehouse doors. He was shouting,

telling his goons to 'get them'! Shalla didn't have to ask who he was talking about. The Rodian and the assassin droid rushed around the side of the building, weapons drawn.

Shalla backed her speeder into the shadows, her fingers clenching around Morq's mane in frustration. The monkey-lizard squeaked in pain as Shalla's lips drew back into a snarl.

Where were those kids?

CHAPTER 9

RESCUE

In a deserted Lothal alleyway, a drain-cover was pushed aside and Milo climbed out. He turned, reaching down into the shaft to recover the box containing CR-8R's head from his sister.

'Any sign of them?' she said, as she pulled herself up into the alley.

Milo looked around. 'Not yet, but they can't be far behind.'

Sure enough, they could soon hear the tramp of running feet and the stomp of a heavy droid.

Milo grabbed Lina's hand and pulled her in the opposite direction.

'How are we going to find Shalla?' she

said, chasing after him.

'We'll work that out when we're safe.'

'Yeah, like we're ever safe these days.'

They made it to the end of the alleyway just as a speeder bike slid across the exit.

'Whoa!' shouted Milo, almost crashing into the bike. 'Watch it, Shalla!'

But it wasn't the owner of the *Moveable Feast*. The rider was a man, with long brown hair and a full beard. The children took one look at him and ran back the way they'd come, only to find themselves cut off by the silhouettes of Rom and IG-70 at the other end of the narrow lane.

They were trapped, again!

'Directive: stay where you are!' boomed the assassin droid, taking a step into the alleyway.

'Yeah, where you are!' repeated Rom, unhelpfully.

Milo squeezed his sister's hand. The guy on the speeder must work for Odai too. They were cornered.

'Well, what are you waiting for?' the bearded man said. 'Hop on!'

Beside Milo, Lina whirled around to face the speeder bike. 'We haven't done anything wrong. Your boss stole Crater's head from *us*, remember!'

'My boss?' The man looked confused. 'Don't you two want to be rescued?'

Milo's head snapped around. 'Rescued?'

'Get on the bike!'

Milo's eyes grew wide. There was something about the voice that he recognised. Something familiar.

'You're the guy from the transmissions!'

'Yes, I am – and if we don't move soon I may never be able to make a transmission again!'

Milo raced forward, breaking Lina's hold on his hand. She paused, but ran to the speeder bike as IG-70 shouted after them.

'Commandment: you will wait!'

'No, we won't,' Milo yelled, jumping onto the bike as Lina climbed on behind.

IG-70 was already shooting as the children's mysterious saviour opened the throttle. The speeder bike shot forward, kicking up dust on the road.

* * *

After dodging in and out of buildings, the speeder bike finally came to a halt outside a nondescript building, no different to the dozens they had already passed.

'Here we are,' said the man, killing the bike's engine.

'We don't even know your name?' said

Milo, sliding off the speeder.

'Inside,' came the only reply, as their rescuer swiped an ID card through a reader on the wall, opening a set of double doors.

Milo glanced at Lina, who shrugged. Neither of them knew if they could trust this guy. He turned back and sighed, guessing what was going on in their heads.

'Look, we can help you, but it isn't safe being on the streets right now.'

'We?'

A female voice came from inside the house, friendly, but concerned: 'Ephraim?'

'Don't worry, it's me,' Ephraim replied. He nodded at Milo and Lina. 'And I brought guests.'

A woman appeared at the door. She was smaller than Ephraim and wore a purple headdress that matched her eyes.

'You found them,' she said, beckoning the children inside. 'Come quickly.'

Realising they didn't have much choice, Milo led the way, still holding the box.

'We've been so worried about you,' the woman said, as Lina crossed the threshold, followed by Ephraim. The door closed behind him.

'You know who we are?' Lina asked.

'You were seen asking questions at the landing strip,' Ephraim explained, locking the door behind him. 'It's just a pity you asked Cikatro Vizago.'

'We've been following your signal, all the way from Thune,' Lina told him.

Ephraim smiled. 'It's reached that far, eh?'

Words spilled out of Milo's mouth. 'Our parents were taken and we didn't know what to do, and then we heard your voice, and–'

'Hush, now,' said the woman, walking over to a table. 'There's plenty of time for all that. Are you hungry? Do you need something to drink?'

Before they could answer, Milo heard a high-pitched giggle. It came from a cot on the other side of the room.

'You've got a baby!' he said, rushing over to see without asking.

'Milo!' Lina warned, but Ephraim laughed.

'It's fine. That's our boy – Ezra.'

Milo looked into the cot to see a chubby infant gazing back up at him with big blue eyes. He had a mop of black hair and reached up with a podgy arm.

Milo reached down and the baby wrapped a tiny hand around his finger. 'He's cute.'

'When he's not screaming the place down,' the woman laughed, joining them beside the crib. 'My name's Mira, and you've already met my husband, Ephraim.'

The bearded man held out his hand to Milo. 'Ephraim Bridger. Pleased to finally make your acquaintance. Sounds like you've been through a lot.'

Mira guided them towards the table and poured glasses of cold blue milk while they told their story.

'And your droid's head is in the box?' Ephraim asked when they'd finished with their narrow escape from Odai's lair.

Lina opened the box to remove CR-8R's head, gently stroking the droid's dormant face. 'And our parent's secrets are in his head.'

'If we'd known what you were getting into, we would have made contact sooner,' Mira said, sadly.

'But we had to be sure,' Ephraim added. 'We're hearing more and more stories like yours – people being taken by Imperial forces; entire families disappearing.'

'It's why we started our broadcasts,' Mira told them. 'To spread hope. It was all we could think to do.'

'And it worked,' cut in Lina, wiping milk from her lip. 'For us, at least. We followed your signal here.'

'Because you hoped we could help

track your parents?' Mira asked.

'Can you?'

The Bridgers looked at each other.

'It may not be as simple as that,' Ephraim said.

'Why?'

'Show them,' Mira said, placing a hand on her husband's arm.

Ephraim nodded and walked over to a circular couch in the corner. He pushed it aside to reveal an open hatch in the floor.

'You'll want to see this,' he said, sitting on the edge of the hole and lowering himself onto a ladder. Milo and Lina crossed over to the hatch, and looked down the deep shaft. Ephraim had reached the bottom. Milo didn't wait. He dropped onto the ladder and climbed down.

'Wow!' he said, finding himself in a hidden room packed with communication equipment. 'Is this where you make the broadcasts?'

'And where we monitor Imperial channels too,' Ephraim confirmed, sitting in front of a large transmitter as Lina joined them. 'The reason we were so cautious is that we've heard that a bounty hunter is on Lothal.' He pressed a control and a hologram appeared above the transmitter. It showed a masked figure. Its glowing eyes seemed to bore straight into Milo.

'Is that him?' Lina asked.

'He's called the Shade,' Ephraim replied. 'No-one knows who's behind the mask,' Ephraim replied. 'We don't even know what's brought him to Lothal, other than it's something big. To be honest, we thought it might be us, but now we know about your droid...'

'You think the Shade's looking for Mum and Dad's data?'

'It's possible. I think we'd better get you off planet.'

'But we've only just arrived,' Milo said. 'We need your help.'

'And that's what you're getting. We can ask around about your parents, but you'll be safer somewhere else, where the Shade can't find you.'

'Can't you tell us anything else about him?'

Ephraim looked doubtful. 'The Shade? There isn't much to tell, other than the fact that he's one of the most dangerous bounty hunters in the Outer Rim. There was something the other day, though.' He continued working the controls, scrolling through files on a screen. 'A deep-space camera picked up an image that may or may not be the Shade's ship, heading this way from Kessel.'

'From Kessel?' Lina asked, frowning.

Ephraim nodded. 'The spice-mine planet, yes.' He found what he was looking for. 'Here it is.'

He pressed a button and the hologram changed. The Shade was replaced by a blurry picture of a speeding freighter in space.

Milo felt his stomach clench.

'What is it?' asked Ephraim, noticing that the colour had drained from Milo's face. 'Do you recognise the ship?'

Milo's mouth was dry, and he couldn't believe what he was seeing. 'Yeah, I do.' He turned to his sister. 'Lina, isn't that the *Moveable Feast*?'

CHAPTER 10

THE GETAWAY

At Twin Horns Storage, Cikatro Vizago was getting tired of being shouted at.

'Where are they?' Rask Odai ranted, almost physically hopping up and down. 'How long does it take to find two children?'

'I'm on this, OK?' Vizago said, holding a communicator to his lips. 'Rom? IG-70? Come in, please. The boss wants a word!'

'A word? I just want my head back!'

'Sounds like you're *losing* your head to me,' Vizago muttered beneath his breath.

'What was that?'

'Nothing boss,' the Devaronian said, talking into the communicator again. 'Rom! IG-70! Where are you?'

'Cikatro Vizago,' said a woman's voice. The horned alien turned to see Shalla Mondatha stroll into the warehouse.

Just when he thought the evening couldn't get any worse. He tried to wave the woman away. 'Not now, eh? Your bugs are safe, but we're closed.' He turned his back on her and called for Rom and IG-70 one last time.

'I don't think they can hear you,' Shalla said, and Vizago jumped as something heavy thudded down at his feet. A tall cylinder rolled across the floor, coming to rest in front of him.

It was IG-70's mechanical head, scorched wires hanging from its neck.

Vizago spun around to find Shalla pointing an energy-bow in his direction

'Where are the children?' she said simply.

'What do you think you're doing?' Odai raged beside Vizago, not used to having his henchman threatened in their own establishment.

'Asking a question,' Shalla replied coolly. 'A question I asked your Rodian and assassin droid a few minutes ago. They answered incorrectly. I suggest you tell me what I want to know.'

'And what's that?' Vizago asked, wondering how quickly he could draw Vilmarh's Revenge.

'The man on the speeder bike, the one who took the children – who is he?'

'We have no idea what you're talking about!' Odai gurgled.

'Wrong answer,' Shalla said, swinging her bow around to shoot one of the golden droids behind the front desk. It exploded in a shower of sparks.

Her weapon was pointing at Vizago again in the blink of an eye.

'Seriously,' the Devaronian said, 'we'd like to find those kids as much as you.' He narrowed his eyes. 'Unless... you know something about the robbery!'

'It was you,' Odai spluttered. 'You were in on it!'

Shalla rolled her eyes. 'Oh, this is taking too long.'

She twisted again, zapping the second droid. Vizago took his chance. He reached for Vilmarh's Revenge, but before he could even slip the blaster from its holster, Shalla had swung her bow towards him and fired.

Vizago screamed as he was thrown back, Vilmarh's Revenge skittering across the floor. His hand shot up to his left horn. The tip was missing! The woman had blown it clean off!

Now Shalla was pointing her bow at Odai. The Mon Calamari was showing his true colours at last, snivelling behind the front desk like the cowardly bully he was.

'Don't shoot,' he begged. 'I'll tell you whatever you want to know, just don't shoot.'

'That's better,' smiled Shalla. 'Now, I'm going to ask you one more time: Who took the children?'

* * *

'You know him?' Ephraim spluttered. 'You know the Shade?'

'Not him,' said Milo. '*Her*. Captain Shalla Mondatha. She's running some kind of cafe down at the landing strip?'

'A *cafe*?'

'It must be a cover,' Lina said.

Ephraim rubbed his hand against his beard. 'And a good one too. What better way to get people talking than to feed them? There's no such thing as a free lunch, after all.'

Lina looked down at her jumpsuit. 'That's why she had all the equipment for the heist. She said it was because she used to be a smuggler.'

'But she's really a bounty hunter,' said Milo. 'Sent to find us!'

'Well, that's what we think,' Ephraim cut in. 'But why not just grab you when she had the chance? Why go through with the robbery?'

'Because it's not us she wants,' Milo realised.

'The data in Crater's head!' Lina said. 'That's why she was helping us. Oh, we're so stupid!'

She thrust her hand into a pocket, pulling out the visor she'd borrowed from Milo in the sewer.

'This thing can transmit,' Lina said. 'That's how she sent us the picture of the keypad.'

'What if it can track as well?' Milo asked.

Ephraim took the visor from her, examining it closely. He sighed. 'You're right. There's a tracker built in.'

'Then she knows we're here!' Milo exclaimed.

Ephraim shook his head. 'Not necessarily.' He looked around the small room. 'This place is shielded.'

'To protect your messages?'

'That's the idea. Our signal is bounced around the local datanet before being broadcast, rather than transmitting direct from our home.'

'So the Empire can't trace the transmission back to the source,' Lina said, completing Ephraim's explanation. 'Clever.'

'And your shield will disrupt the Shade's tracker?' Milo asked.

Now, Ephraim didn't look so sure. 'For now at least. It's not perfect though. The longer you stay here...'

'The more likely it is that she'll find us.'

Lina let out a sigh. 'Then we need to go.'

'I didn't say that,' Ephraim insisted.

'No,' Lina countered. 'But it's true. We can't put you in danger because of us. What you're doing is too important.'

'And there's Ezra too,' Milo

reminded her.

Lina made a decision. 'We need to get back to the *Whisper Bird,* and take off as soon as possible.'

'As long as we have enough fuel,' Milo said. 'Plus, if Shalla's tracking the visor...'

'Then let her follow it,' said Ephraim, grabbing a tool from the table. As the children watched, he pressed it into the side of the glasses, a signal beeping on his transmitter. 'Yes, I thought so.'

He adjusted a control on the transmitter and a holographic map of Capital City appeared in the air, a tiny dot flashing.

'Transmissions work two ways,' he explained. 'That's the Shade, looking for you. Now, if I take this visor over to the other side of town, she'll come running; following me, not you.'

'While we head back to the *Whisper Bird*,' beamed Lina. 'But won't that put you in her firing line?'

'Don't worry about Ephraim,' Mira called down from the top of the ladder. 'He was a bit of a speed demon when he was younger. He can outrace anyone.'

Ephraim led them back up into the lounge. 'I'm just sorry we can't do more. Once you've got away, we'll start looking for your parents, and be in touch.'

'You should take this too,' said Mira, pushing a bag into Lina's hands, 'To buy more fuel. I'm just sorry it's not more.'

Lina looked inside. It was full of credits. 'We can't take this.'

'You can, and you must. Do you know the way back to the landing strip from here?'

Lina nodded as Milo grabbed CR-8R's head. 'I think so.'

'Then we need to go,' Ephraim said, making for the door. 'It's dark out there, but the moons should give you enough light. You need to get off Lothal as soon as you can!'

* * *

Neither Lina or Milo spoke as they ran along the Lothal streets. They tried to stay in the long shadows cast by the skyscrapers, although the tall towers didn't look so beautiful anymore.

They stopped with every transport that passed, jumping into doorways and behind stalls, imagining Shalla jumping out of them at every turn.

No, not Shalla. The Shade. They didn't even know if Shalla was her real name.

The *Whisper Bird* was waiting for them when they made it to the landing strip. The *Moveable Feast* was beside it, but the Shade's craft was shut up, no lights blazing through its portholes.

Clutching CR-8R's head, Milo raced for the *Bird,* only stopping when he heard an excited cry. He turned to see Morq, crouched below a nearby speeder bike.

'There you are,' Milo said, running to his pet. 'I was scared she'd hurt you. Come on, we need to get on board the *Bird.*'

Morq didn't move. He just sat there, quivering.

'What's wrong with him?' asked Lina, coming up behind Milo. That was when she noticed the collar around Morq's thin neck. It was connected to a chain that in turn was lashed to the speeder bike.

'I wondered if you'd come back for him,' said a voice from behind. It was Shalla, standing beneath the nose of the *Whisper Bird.* She was still wearing her knitted shawl, but now it was covering black body armour rather than overalls.

'I suppose I don't need this anymore,' she said, unfastening the shawl at her neck. 'You don't look very pleased to see me, after all.'

'We know who you are!' Lina shouted back, standing shoulder by shoulder with her brother. 'You're a bounty hunter – the Shade.'

'Am I now?' Shalla asked, turning the shawl inside out. The other side of the fabric was dark and smooth, like a cloak. She draped it over her shoulders again, fixing the clasp beneath her chin.

'Where's your mask?' Milo asked, trying to sound threatening. Lina wasn't sure it worked.

Shalla cocked her head. 'I can put it on if you want? Perhaps after you've given me that head.'

'No,' Lina said, standing in front of Milo. 'We won't.'

'I thought you'd say that. It was clever, ditching the visor. Whoever rescued you obviously still thinks I'm chasing it around town.'

'We found your signal,' Lina insisted.

'No, you found a tracker stuck to the back of a Wakizan beetle. As soon as I realised that Odai didn't have you, I knew you'd come back for your ship. So I prepared a little welcome home surprise for you.' Shalla pulled out a gloved hand. She was holding her datapad. 'Either you surrender, or I press this button.'

'And what will that do?' Milo asked.

'Oh, nothing much,' said Shalla. 'Just detonate the thermo-grenade I've hidden on that speeder bike. You know, the one chained to your little pet!'

Milo turned to face Morq who was staring at them with wide, frightened eyes. 'You can't! He hasn't done anything to you!'

'I can and I will,' Shalla insisted. 'So what's it going to be, Milo: Surrender, or bye-bye Morq?'

* * *

Ephraim Bridger pulled up alongside the landing strip, killing his speeder bike's engines. It had soon become clear that the Shade wasn't following him, so he had taken the fight to her, tracking her signal to an alleyway not far from Twin Horns Storage.

He'd eventually found the tracker stud on the back of a particularly nasty-looking insect. She'd tricked them.

But perhaps the children had

reached their ship before she'd found them, perhaps they'd got away. He'd check and then get back to Mira. There was only one problem. He had no idea what their ship looked like.

There was one he recognised though – the *Moveable Feast*.

The Shade's ship.

A sudden movement caught his eye. Someone was walking from behind the bird-like ship next to the *Feast*.

His heart sank when he saw who it was.

Milo and Lina Graf were being led towards the *Feast* by a figure in a long cloak. Ephraim pulled out a pair of electrobinoculars and took a closer look. Yes, it was a woman, with CR-8R's head tucked beneath her arm. He checked the *Feast*'s ramp, spotting a droid's headless body already loaded onboard the ship.

He lowered the binoculars. Could he stop them before they took off?

It was doubtful. Even if he moved quickly, there was no guarantee that the Shade wouldn't hurt the children. Besides, Ephraim was no fighter. He knew that.

But he had friends who were.

Grimly, he watched as the party

marched up the ramp. It raised with the sound of hydraulic gears, and seconds later, the *Feast*'s engines roared. A cloud of dirt billowed from beneath the freighter as it rose into the air, only to sweep overhead and blast high into the sky a moment later.

Ephraim pulled a communicator from his tunic and opened a channel.

'Ryder, it's me... Yes, I know you told me not to call you just yet, but this is important. We need to mount a rescue.'